To Cyndi –
Love, Mum + Jon

Praise for "The Listening Tree"

"Your stories are really life-filled and uplifting. Thanks for sending them along. You should consider publishing them, if there is a market for such."
—Reverend Charles R. Mallen, C.S.S.R., director, Our Lady of Perpetual Help Retreat and Spirituality Center, Venice, Florida

"I thought your writings were fine, sensitive, intelligent and revealing."
—Monsignor Robert W. Schiefen, pastor, St. Isabel, Sanibel Island, Florida, (deceased)

"I firmly believe that those who have made your type of journey ultimately end by making the greatest contributions on behalf of the kingdom."
—Very Reverend Gerard LaCerra, V.G.,chancellor, Archdiocese of Miami, (deceased).

"You are so rare and special. You have shown the family what no words can speak. Not a day goes by that I don't talk about you in some positive way. I pray I can pass on to your grandchildren all these lessons, patience and love you have given me."
—Mary Charlene Nishida, director of corporate and foundation relations, American Cancer Society Hawaii Pacific, Inc.

"Deborah and I have read your stories and poems and find them beautifully written. I will put them in the bookstore for our parishioners."
——Reverend Bob Deshaies, rector, St. Benedict's Episcopal Church, Plantation, Florida.

The Listening Tree

Fifty Stories of Grace-full Everyday Living

Joyce Ann Edmondson

PublishAmerica
Baltimore

First printing

Biblical references are from The New American Bible, copyright Catholic Publishers, Inc. 1971, and the Holy Bible, King James Version, American Bible Society, copyright 1990.

ISBN: 1-4137-3761-7
PUBLISHED BY PUBLISHAMERICA, LLLP
www.publishamerica.com
Baltimore

Printed in the United States of America

Dedication

Our Mother of Perpetual Help
and
parents and grandparents everywhere

Contents

The Listening Tree

"…And it grew and became a large tree, and the birds of the air nested in its branches…" Luke 13:19

A large oak tree grows in the schoolyard at Gratigny Elementary School in North Miami, Florida. The faces of the children who seek shade under its branches have darkened over the years since Charlene and Sue first climbed into its arms in the seventies to reveal their childhood prophesies. A twister uprooted the old tree, but caretakers replanted it and now the tree lives on, year after year, listening to the children's secrets, while enfolding them in its protective arms.

Charlene and Sue sat on a limb high in the tree and recorded their conversation on a tape recorder they had received at Christmas.

"Did you know that animals are more important than people because the animals were invented first?" said Sue emphatically.

She continued, "and dinosaurs are no longer on the earth because the people shot them all."

Charlene replied, "there is a certain type of bird that used to live on the earth—there were probably thousands of them—and then there was only one because the people killed them, and he probably died by now."

A breeze rustled the leaves in the old tree as Sue related with concern, "When our children grow up there probably won't be any animals left, and our children will have to read about them in books, and they won't believe it anyway because they won't see them— they'll have to pray to God to send more animals, and if you were a bear and somebody shot you, well, how would you like it? You probably wouldn't like it at all, would you? And bears are just like us except they don't think like us."

To whom were they speaking, these children just entering into the ecological consciousness of a nation? Were they repeating their concern, or a national concern they had absorbed from others?

"If you don't get married you can be somebody special, like a nun or widow," Charlene responded eagerly.

Sue grew somber, "your children will have to wear dresses three times a week and twice on Sunday."

"You can be a martyr," she stated enthusiastically, "by letting someone shoot you instead of the fox because if there are no animals, the people will die!"

Charlene mused, "Allessandro was forgiven by Maria Goretti for murdering her, became a priest and when he died, forgave God for everything."

The old tree shuddered at the thought, while his branches shook with laughter. The tree seemed to agree "eye has not seen, nor ear heard, nor has it entered into the heart what God has prepared for his children, except the Spirit show them." But it rejoiced for the things hidden from the wise and learned and revealed to the childlike.

"Blessed are those who trust in the Lord, and whose hope is the Lord. For they shall be like a tree planted by the waters, which spreads out its roots by the river, and will not fear when heat comes; but its leaf will be green, and will not be anxious in the year of drought, nor will cease from yielding fruit." Jeremiah 17:7-8

The Rose Garden

When Grandmother was a young girl she was often invited to her aunt and uncle's farm in southern Florida for two or three weeks each summer. Her uncle was a lawyer by profession and a gentleman farmer by preference. There were citrus and nut groves, vegetable gardens, chickens, pigs, cows, and in hunting season rabbit and quail. On the front lawn there was a manmade pond with the shiny scales of goldfish glistening in the sunshine and on the porch a swing from which she loved to stretch her legs back and forth on hot summer days.

Aunt Jessie served fresh vegetables for dinner and supper (terms for lunch and dinner in the south), made sausage, scrapple and biscuits, churned butter, gathered eggs from the hen house and fried chicken every Sunday, after which there would be bowls of freshly made ice cream made from real cream and flavored with fresh strawberries from the field.

One day Grandmother asked her aunt if she believed in God. Aunt Jessie's response was to take the little girl by the hand and lead her to the rose garden in which she had planted many varieties of roses with mellifluous odors and vibrant hues. Aunt Jessie answered her, "God is everywhere," and Grandmother believed it with all her heart and soul.

Grandmother's own mother was often very sick, and when she was in bed, Aunt Jessie would take the little girl home to the farm, buy her school clothes, get her hair permed in another aunt's beauty salon and go grocery shopping with her to purchase the items she needed not available on the farm.

When they arrived back home, she would watch Aunt Jessie grab a live chicken, twist its head off, wait for it to stop hopping around as

11

the nerves died, put it in boiling water, pluck its feathers, cut it up and fry it. All seemed natural to Grandmother at the time, although years later after living in the city, it was an unpleasant memory.

Her uncle would take her on his truck to the nut groves where they would gather pecans, and to the citrus groves for tangerines, grapefruit and oranges. Sometimes she would accompany her aunt or uncle to gather vegetables, one time cutting her thumb on a razor sharp leaf from a stalk of corn. She gathered eggs with her aunt and stood by her side while she milked a cow, which kicked Grandmother when she tried to milk it, much to her fright. She was very embarrassed when her uncle who was somewhat of a tease, named a pig after her.

It was the custom, at a dinner table served by a maid, to pass the empty plates around and stack them when the meal was finished. However, when company would come, Aunt Jessie would have the maid pick up each individual plate from the table. One day, not knowing if the guests were company or family, the maid whispered in Aunt Jessie's ear, "Mam, is they company, or does we stack?"

During the World War II years, her father, also a lawyer by profession, was out of work. Grandmother was very sick with the flu and there was no food in the house. Her aunt brought potatoes, carrots and beets from the farm and cooked them in a large pot, serving them to her with melted butter from the farm. Grandmother thought she had never tasted so delicious a meal.

When Aunt Jessie was a young married lady, it was not the custom for black servants to eat with the family. Many black families remained on the farms and plantations after the Civil War days and worked on the family land. Many also left, went to schools and colleges, and owned and operated businesses.

Following the custom of the time in the South, Aunt Jessie served meals to the black housemaids or workers on the back porch, but she had never approved of the custom. When she grew old and hardening of the arteries affected her memory, she forgot the customs of the past and invited her servants to eat with the family at the dining room table. The goodness of her heart overcame the weakness of her body and mind as she aged. She became one of the beautiful roses in her garden tended by God, who she believed was everywhere.

The kingdom of God is like a good aunt who feeds you when you are hungry, visits you when you are sick, takes care of you and teaches you about God. She invites you to find God in everything and everyone. In your memory she is a sweet-smelling rose in God's garden and she draws you to her and teaches you to trust in life.

Baptism by Immersion

When Grandmother was thirteen years old, her best friend told her that if she was not baptized she would go to hell, and she would not be her friend anymore. Grandmother did not have any concept of what hell was. She had not been taught a specific faith, but she knew what it meant to lose a friend, so she agreed to be baptized in the Baptist Church.

Grandmother asked the minister of the church she had been attending with her friend to baptize her. He told her to come to church the next Sunday evening and he would baptize Grandmother, but he did not explain what it meant or how he would do it. Grandmother arrived at the church and was told to walk down a long, dark hallway, at the end of which was a door. When she opened the door she walked down several steps into a pool of water where the minister was waiting for her. He took her forehead, leaned her head back and immersed her in the water. Poor Grandmother had not known that she would be baptized in this way and when she came up from the water she was laughing from the shock. Her Sunday school teacher, who was in the congregation watching her, scolded her later for laughing.

Grandmother tried very hard to be a good Baptist, but the church did not approve of dancing, and it seemed to Grandmother, who liked to dance, that God might have other plans for her. When she became a Catholic ten years later, she remembered the experience and learned what the signs of Baptism meant. She learned that going down into the water represents one form of Baptism and is a sign of dying in Christ, and coming out of the water, rising to new life in Him. The white dress she made and wore when she received Holy Communion for the first time was a sign of God's grace and that she was cleansed from original sin and any personal sins she had committed.

Grandmother sent the white dress to the missions so another girl like Grandmother could use it when she was baptized. Grandmother thought she was very fortunate to have an opportunity to learn what it meant to be a Christian. She thanked God for the gift of faith for which she had prayed when she was 16 years old.

If hell is the absence of God, not having Jesus as your best friend is a pretty good description. So, heaven is being friends with God. There are many ways we may choose to keep Jesus as our friend in this life, and live forever with Him in the next.

Sixteen

In the summer of 1949, just before her seventeenth birthday, Grandmother got a job as receptionist in the hospital where she was born. The family moved into a small cottage and rented their home to save money to send Grandmother to college. Her salary was needed for living expenses for the family, as her father could not find enough work for his legal practice. Her mother was very sick, and Grandmother did not know this was how they planned to pay her college tuition.

Grandmother's search for her vocation or purpose in life began sometime during that summer. She spent her days receiving patients into the hospital, but her evenings were spent in reading. Her home had always been filled with books. She had read many of the classics of the time: "The Bobsy Twins," "The Secret Garden," Sherlock Holmes mysteries, a set of Harvard Classics, and sometimes she would open the Bible to any page and start reading, a practice she would later scorn. So far, no one had explained anything about the Bible or religion to her. That particular summer, however, a friend had given her the book "The Big Fisherman," and she was immersed in reading the life of Jesus and portrayal of Peter.

The situation at home seemed desperate and compelling to her. She felt she had no faith or hope in her present situation. She sought with her whole being to know her own destiny and purpose in life. It came to her in a vision as she silently prayed and begged God to reveal Himself and His plans to her. As she prayed, for a moment she saw before her a figure of light, while words formed inwardly in her mind as individual concepts, "You…will…help…your…family." Grandmother was frightened and screamed for her mama, who came to her bedside and told her it was a dream. Grandmother knew she had not been asleep, and from this event the direction for her life had come to her in an extraordinary way in answer to her prayer.

Throughout her life, Grandmother's sustaining hope and faith had always been to help her family, even when she did not know who her family was. She always dedicated herself unreservedly to the task before her depending on the grace of God.

When we pray, we give our whole attention to God. He becomes present to us just as if we were with our best friend discussing our most secret thoughts. Then God speaks with us in our minds and hearts. We listen very carefully to what He is revealing to us. He speaks with us through our parents, teachers and lawful authority, but He will speak with you in your heart in the privacy of your room if you pray to Him. Sometimes words are not enough. We want tangible proof of His existence and concern for us. Then we may look out at the earth's beauty, or power in a storm, or in the eyes of a friend. God speaks to us through each of these as well. God speaks to us in church through His Word. Then we offer God a gift that represents ourselves and He gives Jesus back to us. The Mass is the best prayer we have, because in the Mass, Jesus offers Himself and all of us to His Father, and we receive Him back in Holy Communion to take with us into our lives. There is no greater proof of God's love for each individual person than His death on the cross. If you feel you do not know God or what He wants you to do, pray to Him as a friend and He will answer you.

"Ask and it will be given to you; seek and you will find; knock and the door will be opened to you. For everyone who asks, receives; and the one who seeks, finds; and to the one who knocks, the door will be opened..." Matthew 7:7-8

Violets in the Snow

One year after high school graduation, Grandmother's parents sent her to a work-study college in Yellow Springs, Ohio. She was a Southern girl who had lived in Florida all of her life. She had never seen autumn leaves or snow. In Antioch College she saw leaves turn to gold, orange, red and brown. She learned how to take beeswax, melt it in a pot of boiling water, dip the leaves in the wax, and dry them. Grandmother mailed the leaves home to her mother.

One day in early November it got very cold, the sky turned grey, and snowflakes began to drift softly down. After several hours, about six inches of snow had fallen. Grandmother became very excited and went for a walk with other students in the glen near the college. Some of the students took cardboard boxes, tore them apart and used them to sit on and slide down the hill into the deepening snow. After a while, Grandmother became enchanted by the untouched purity of the virgin snow in the woodland area and decided to explore it herself. She walked deeper and deeper into the woods, observing the pure white snow, the delicate bird tracks, and experiencing the stillness around her. As she walked on, mesmerized by the beauty of her surroundings, she became aware she had lost her way and was frightened. After what seemed a very long time she found her way back to the college where her friends were snuggled down in a nice warm dorm, playing on the guitar and singing folk songs. She was relieved to be back.

In three months Grandmother traveled to New York City for her "work experience," part of the college five-year program for all students. The pure white snow turned to a dirty slush in the city, Grandmother's own mother died, and her money ran out. Nevertheless, after the funeral service she returned to the city and remained there for five more years, until one year the violets of a new spring season pushed their way through the sidewalk cracks in Central Park, and new life appeared everywhere.

Grandmother had grown tired of the city where she had not been able to find what she was looking for, and was unable to help her remaining family. She was homesick for a warmer climate and her father's house. So the prodigal daughter returned home, where God was waiting for her with open arms. Broken in spirit, God's grace found a way into her soul and she went to live with a Christian family of the Catholic faith for a year. There she helped the family with their five children and absorbed whatever faith they taught her through their actions, without being able to say what it was.

Sometimes bad things happen to good people, but God will always be with us to bring good out of evil, and give us sufficient grace to live with Him here and in heaven. God is so good He will never let anything happen to us that can't be fixed. If it can't be fixed here on this earth, if we accept His will for us, God will fix it in heaven.

Chosen

When Grandmother first met Father Charlie, she had never before come face to face with a priest of the Roman Catholic Church. In high school, a priest came once a year, along with other ministers, and gave a talk to the student assembly. She remembered that all the Catholic students were always excited when his turn came. Grandmother was unprepared for the encounter with Father Charlie, thinking he was an angel or someone from an unknown planet. She innocently asked him who he was. He told her simply that he was a priest of the Catholic Church, but followed that statement with another that startled Grandmother who was not of a specific faith.

Grandmother was living with a Catholic family and Father Charlie visited from time to time. He would take all the five children and Grandmother to a skating rink where he taught her to skate. She had been gradually absorbing the gift of faith from the family through their actions and words. Father Charlie knew how to relate to people. When he came to their home he would sing songs with them, play with the children, and eat what they ate. At the time of this encounter with Father Charlie, Grandmother had not verbalized her response to his words.

"You should belong to some kind of faith," he told her. "I don't care what faith, but some kind, or you will not make it in life."

She replied to him, "I'll never be anything but a Catholic." Years later Grandmother would include other branches of the Catholic Church and Christians in her life, but at the time she was only referring to the Roman Catholic Church.

Grandmother soon found a job in a Catholic summer camp in San Antonio, Florida with the Benedictine nuns. There she learned what life as a Sister in a community was like. When she returned from the summer camp, she took instructions in the church and was baptized again conditionally, a custom not followed today because most forms of Baptism are now considered valid.

Father Charlie provided guidance, direction, confidence and affection at the time she needed it most. He was like the Good Shepherd who left the ninety-nine sheep and went to claim a lost lamb for God. God said that those who leave family, home and possessions for the kingdom of God to serve Him would be rewarded a hundred-fold and life eternal. He also said, "Many are called, but few are chosen." Yet each person is chosen to make Christ's presence known to the others who come into their lives. "Bloom where you are planted," is a saying Grandmother believed.

Later on in her life, Grandmother went to visit Father Charlie in the retreat center he and others had founded. He told her at that time God had created him to be a Father. He reminded her the most important day in her life was the day she was baptized and always to remember that. Grandmother asked him what he was going to do with all the treasure he was collecting in heaven. He answered, "I will share it with my friends." This is what it means to be chosen by God to be a Father and be His living word on this earth. Father Charlie was a living word in God's kingdom. His mission was to show what God was like, just as Jesus did.

Religious people are not perfect. They are human, but they allow God to work on their imperfections and ask Him to change their hearts, just as everyone else does. Father Charlie had one imperfection. He had hugged so many people in his life that his arms had grown longer and longer, and they could reach around many people at the same time. Every time he hugged his friends (and sometimes his enemies) his heart grew a little larger and his arms a little longer. Of course, this is only a symbolic way of saying that he had a heart for loving and arms for embracing the people of God, which he did through his prayer life and actions. He once told Grandmother, "A celibate is someone who loves all people equally."

Grandmother thanked God every day for introducing her to Father Charlie and bringing her into His kingdom—already here, not yet.

If God Made the World, How Can it be Bad?

The first nun that Grandmother met at the age of 23 was a Benedictine nun named Sister Irma. Sister Irma had magnificent, large, round blue eyes which pierced into Grandmother's soul and read her mind, or so it seemed to her. She floated rather than walked, and the first time Grandmother spoke with her, Sister Irma quoted the Ten Commandments backwards. When she got to the first commandment, "I am the Lord your God. You shall not have false gods before me…" all the false gods Grandmother had previously worshiped, such as beautiful dresses and boyfriends, fell away and the one true God stood before her in a slender nun with piercing blue eyes. Or so it seemed to Grandmother.

Not long after their first meeting, Sister Irma sent Grandmother into a first grade classroom to relieve the teacher, also a nun. A small child was reading from a book in such a soft voice Grandmother couldn't hear her. She asked the child to read louder. At the second request, she felt a tugging on her dress. A little girl looked up at her and said, "Why don't you go and stand next to her." This was the first lesson Grandmother learned from her future students, but it was not to be the last.

One day when she was teaching third grade, a freckle-faced, redheaded boy was misbehaving in the water line and Grandmother told him to go to the end of the line. He was back by her side almost immediately, looked up at her and mischievously remarked, "I went to the end of the line like you said, but there was somebody already there!" Then he and Grandmother and the entire class started laughing. He told her his father had taught him that one.

The summer after her first teaching experience as third grade teacher in Jacksonville, Florida, Grandmother spend three months at the Benedictine mother house in San Antonio, Florida, as arts and crafts instructor of the summer camp program. At this time she began to contemplate becoming a nun. The following summer she told the mother superior, who advised her it would be best to wait another year since she was a new convert to the faith. At the end of the next year, however, she advised Grandmother she believed she had a vocation in the world, not the convent. Grandmother wished she had told her in the beginning. She did not know how Mother Superior knew this, but accepted it as one of the mysteries of the Church. She understood how you discover a vocation is to think about it, pray for God's will, and talk with a priest or sister, seek admission and wait for the answer. This time the answer was "no." God had other plans for her. Grandmother spent the next seven years teaching before she met and married her future husband.

When she moved to Miami and taught in Our Lady of Perpetual School, her friend, Father Charlie, told her these would be the best years of her life. Not believing Mother Superior or Father Charlie, Grandmother applied to two more religious orders and each told her she had a vocation in the world to serve God. Finally, Grandmother accepted God's plan for her and began to adjust. She devoted her time and energy to Christian action and teaching until she met her husband-to-be, the grandfather of Nicholas. Grandmother thought life in the world would be difficult, but she loved God and wanted what He wanted for her.

Jesus said we must carry our own cross each day if we want to live with Him. There is no other way to the kingdom but through Jesus. In Baptism, we die with Jesus in order to be raised up by God in everlasting life with Him. Now that we know there are millions, perhaps, of other solar systems with planets traveling in them, we realize not only is the universe infinitely bigger than we can imagine, but our time on this earth is like a drop in the ocean compared with life eternal. No matter what God asks of us, if we accept it and make the best of it, our cross will be light as a feather because He will be carrying it with us.

The Brave Sisters

Grandmother had been a teacher in Our Lady of Perpetual Help School in Opa Locka, Florida for about six years. A group of sisters of the Holy Names of Jesus and Mary, in charge of the school, had been traveling home from holiday via the old trail that was surrounded by canals on both sides. The car had suddenly veered from the narrow highway off into the water, with five or six sisters going down with it. As related later by the surviving sisters, the driver's body had been thrust against the power window button and the window went down just before the car entered the water. The driver was able to get out and seek help. The two older sisters managed to survive long enough to push the younger ones through the window, thus saving their lives, but they were not able to get out and died by drowning.

Grandmother's eyes still filled with tears when she remembered the brave sisters who chose death by immersion to save the lives of the others.

First Runner-up

When Grandpa was in his twenties, he thought he had a vocation to become a priest, so he entered the Trappist monastery at Gethsemane. After a few years, the abbot told him he did not have a vocation to be a priest, but could remain as a brother. Grandpa decided he did not want to be a brother, so he left.

While in the monastery, Grandpa met Thomas Merton, a now famous Trappist monk and author. Grandpa said he had never spoken with Thomas Merton in words because at the time they were only allowed to speak in sign language, except at certain times. He described the sign language as a combination of "monastery" and signing. Grandpa's parents were both deaf and mute, so he was very familiar with the language of the monastery.

Grandpa said Merton was a very humble man. He suffered from ulcers, Grandpa said, but he never complained. He was writing at the time, but went into the fields with all the other monks. His writing was secondary to his religious life. His prayer life and relationship with God came first, Grandpa said.

After Grandpa left the monastery, he came to Miami where he met and married Grandmother. After their two children were born, he was fixing the roof on their home and fell off a ladder and injured himself. While recuperating from the accident, he became restless and started taking their children, Jim and Charlene, to track meets where he trained them to run races. Both were very fast runners and when clocked in an official AAU track meet, set world records for their age group and were written up in the Miami Herald.

It was at that time Grandpa began visiting young people in Youth Hall who had gotten into trouble with the law. Charlene wrote about her father in a college scholarship competition at St. Thomas University in which she placed "first runner-up," thus insuring her college education.

"When I reminisce about my past, I recall some truly grand times. Both my parents are naturals when it comes to dealing with kids. My father was the founder of Hall of Fame, Inc., a non-profit program dealing with teenagers with some type of drug problem. The program encouraged them to make their bodies useful, not waste them.

"My mother was the first person to organize Vacation Bible School in our parish. Our family had also been involved at a group home in which we gave kids a second chance. I was taught at an early age to accept responsibility, to make choices and decisions based on their effect and outcome. I have learned to think about other people and put myself second. By helping others, I help myself. Since I was exposed to stress at such an early age, I can handle big doses of it. I know how to face reality and keep my own dreams in mind. For two years I was a Sunday school teacher, not for the orderly students, but for the ones the teachers felt were uncontrollable, the ones that were a disturbance in class. I cannot say exactly how I will help my community. I know I want to help. My eagerness is unyielding and I can guarantee that I am a risk worth investing in. After all, as I have learned, isn't that what life is about—taking risks?"

Charlene was graduated with honors at St. Thomas University and has worked to help people ever since. She began her career in Colorado and, using her marketing degree, moved to San Francisco, California where she worked for the Girl Scout council at a time when the state had no funds for art, music or physical education. They provided an interim program for the children. When she moved to Hawaii, she worked for a hospice and trained volunteers to work with the dying.

Grandpa's son, Jim, became a petty officer on board the U.S.S. Nimitz, where he worked with computers, as a supervisor. Today he is the proud father of three children, Nicholas, Kyra and Dawson.

Grandmother thought about the training Grandpa had given his children in the track program and with the teenagers. It was a risk worth taking!

Charlene received her first Holy Communion in St. James Parish, North Miami, Florida. A reading from the letter of Paul to the Philippians was the second reading at the Mass.

"It is not that I have reached it yet, or have already finished my course; but I am racing to grasp the prize, if possible, since I have been grasped by Jesus Christ. Brothers, I do not think of myself as having reached the finish line. I give no thought to what lies behind, but push on to what is ahead. My entire attention is on the finish line as I run toward the prize to which God calls me—life on high in Christ Jesus. This is the Word of the Lord."

Shells on the Beach

People from all over the world came to the tiny island of Sanibel, Florida to gather shells of many varieties and sizes that had washed up on shore and covered the beaches. When Grandmother and her family went on vacation to Sanibel Island they discovered that over the years many shells had been removed. They were so few and far between, except out on the reef where a boat would have to take them.

A native islander told them about a secret beach on the island where shells were plentiful. He politely shared information and directions that the family followed faithfully. Arriving on the beach, they found mounds and mounds of shells and not a single person bothering to gather them. They walked up and down the beach until late in the afternoon picking up the most beautiful shells and bringing them back to the car to take home.

When the family returned home they washed all the sand from the shells, scrubbed and polished them and brought them into the house. Then they made shell lamps and mirrors, and put them in a fish tank to look at and enjoy. These items brought back pleasant memories of their trip to Sanibel Island for many years, until the children were grown.

The kingdom of Heaven is like a beautiful beach where thousands and thousands of shells sparkle in the sun and you, your family, Jesus and all your friends can gather all that your heart desires, as long as you wish.

The Pearl

Grandmother believed there is a precious pearl being formed in everyone's life. Like the sand slowly but surely forms the pearl in the oyster, all the circumstances of life under God's grace form this pearl. Often the pearl is hidden and we don't know it is there, but when we search we will find it.

Jesus said when we find the pearl, we will want to sell everything we have to purchase it. Jesus was not talking about material possessions, Grandmother thought, but getting rid of everything that makes the pearl lose its luster, chip, or erode it and make it valueless.

Grandmother knew a couple who were like precious pearls hidden in the ocean of God's love. They were the godparents of Grandmother's children, Charlene and Jim. They had eight children of their own, and when they were born each child in turn received the name of a saint from the Old Testament all the way into the New: Joseph, David, Mary, Julie, Thomas, Therese, Chris Edel, and John. Esther and her husband, David Sr., gave each of their children a Catholic school education, including college, if they wanted it. They lived simply without many of the material luxuries of today's society, devoted time to serve their parish family, were always friends to the poor and homeless, including Grandmother and her children at times. They did not travel the world or spread the Gospel in foreign missions because they were home raising their children, but each child possessed a missionary spirit which sought to share the faith with others or touch the lives of those who needed to know Christ better. Each child became a jewel or a pearl in Esther and David's crown.

Grandmother sat down on the sofa in the living room and thought about Esther and David and the beautiful crowns they would wear in heaven, with rubies, diamonds, sapphires, and precious pearls. She saw in her imagination God placing the crowns lovingly on their heads and saying to them, "Well done, beloved friends, welcome to my kingdom. When I was hungry, you gave me food; thirsty, you gave me drink; naked, and you clothed me; sick, you visited me." They looked at Jesus and asked, "Lord, when did we do these things?" Jesus replied, "When you did it for the least of your and my little ones, you did it for me. Welcome, welcome, welcome to my home." Then they will all sit down together and exchange family stories.

"Again, the kingdom of Heaven is like a merchant searching for fine pearls. When he finds a pearl of great price, he goes and sells all that he has and buys it." Matthew 13:45-46

On Stores and Garage Sales

In her early married years, Grandmother's sister and brother-in-law owned stores in Provincetown, Cape Cod, and Sarasota, Florida. In her later years she bought "things" for the stores she no longer owned. She would collect these treasures, keep them for a while, and then bring them to Grandmother's house to sort through and decide if she wanted to keep or sell them in a garage sale. Grandmother often attempted a sale, but her sister would come to the sale, reclaim the items, and the sale couldn't take place. Sometimes, Grandmother would buy her sister's treasures, which always found their way back to the next sale. They played this game for several years, until they both realized what was happening. After that they would simply collect the items and take them to a Goodwill box for disposition, which saved them a lot of trouble.

Grandmother's sister, Marilyn, had lived in the country most of her life. When her daughter, Carrie Anne, was six years old, they moved to Miami near Grandmother. One day Carrie Anne, familiar with country lingo, told her mother and aunt she knew where she could buy "live peeps" (baby chicks) for 50 cents apiece. Grandmother looked a little askance, but thought no more about it as Marilyn and Carrie Anne climbed into their car to go after their prize chicks. Now, the store where Grandmother's niece had seen the sign was on Seventh Avenue in the North Miami section of town, and it occurred to Grandmother that she had never seen a store selling baby peeps there herself. As told by her sister when they returned, they had driven along Seventh Avenue and soon came to a bar with a sign reading "Live peeps—50 cents." Marilyn had to sadly explain to

Carrie Anne what "live peeps" means in the city. Grandmother was very sad to see the expression on her niece's face and to know that she had probably encountered her first experience with the "evils" of city living.

In the kingdom of God, He will restore and preserve our innocence and we will see everything through His eyes. There will be no double meanings. Whatever is good and pure and holy in all of creation will never be changed or corrupted again.

U.S.S. Nimitz

When Grandmother's son, Jim, was 18 years old, he left his home in Miami and joined the Navy. First, he went into basic training and then to Norfolk, Virginia, for training as a petty officer. His first assignment was aboard the U.S.S. Nimitz carrier, one of the largest nuclear aircraft carriers in the fleet. In a letter home he described his life, a portion of which follows:

"...The ship is getting ready for O.R.E. (Operational Readiness Exam). This exam determines how well the crew is ready for such things as nuclear attacks, chemical and biological attacks, and missile attacks. Also, how well we react to fires, mass casualties, torpedo hits and medical emergencies. We have this drill all day, every day. They come over the ship's intercom and announce G.Q. (General Quarters) and everybody must go to their G.Q. station in a hurry. Mine is on the flight deck. I'm a stretcher-bearer. That is, we carry the injured to medical facility. You never know whether it's a drill or for real. Already there have been some severe accidents and some of the crew have come close to death. One man lost his legs in an aircraft elevator accident. It's so dangerous around here. You must look out and be aware wherever you are, especially the men working on the flight deck. During drills it's so loud up there I can't stand it. Sometimes aircraft are taking off and landing. I really feel sorry for those guys. They work 14-18 hour days. Sometimes I find them taking a break and I look at them and they're in trances from fatigue, long hours, the heat and loudness. They really get strung out. The other day an E-2 Hawkeye was coming in for landing, and it's really difficult for pilots to land on an aircraft carrier. It bounced off the deck, hit four other aircraft with its wing and took off again with part of it wing missing. They say it's a miracle that the airplane didn't go into the water. Anyway, they didn't think the aircraft could come back around and try to land again, and being thousands of miles from land, it couldn't make it to land. So, they tried it again and made it. Only one person got hurt. It doesn't make any sense how man can go to such great lengths to make military powers so great at the cost of men's lives. Millions of dollars are spent, a massive amount of weapons made to fight one another and kill one another, when peace is so much easier and less expensive."

Grandmother was proud of her son and the way he thought. When she was a young teacher she rode a city bus to the movies because she didn't have a car. While she was riding, she thought about the boys at war (then Vietnam) and realized that only because of young men defending our country did she have the freedom to ride across town to a movie. Yet, she did not understand why they were at war at the time, and she did not believe many of her son's Navy buddies did either. War is a complex concept, and now that she had a son in the Navy who was only a boy a few years ago, she began to realize how Mary, the Mother of Jesus, must have felt when her Son went out into the world to do His Father's will, even when it meant His Life.

Jim remained in the Navy for six years aboard the U.S.S. Nimitz and then returned home to his family with an honorable discharge. He had gone around the world three times, had seen countries and places his parents would never see; had visited Rome, The Vatican, met with the Pope, visited Jerusalem and the Holy Land, yet in his heart he longed to put his feet on dry land and drive a car again. He had been 18, only a boy, when he left home; now he was a man.

The gifts of the Spirit give us the courage and fortitude to do God's will, no matter how difficult. Confirmation gives us special strength to live our faith, and by word and action to be true witnesses of Christ. Just as each man in the Navy has a special uniform, we receive a spiritual seal that marks us as Christians. We receive the gifts of wisdom, understanding, right judgment, courage, knowledge, reverence and holy fear (respect) in God's presence.

Giving Thanks

When Grandmother and Grandpa worked for the state of Florida as foster parents of young teenagers who were first offenders, they had their hands full. Their own children were young at the time and relatively easy to manage, but the teenagers were older and needed a lot of understanding, support and love since they had gotten themselves in trouble with the law for the first time. Grandpa related well with teens and thought he could help them. He had been visiting in Youth Hall when the state of Florida began a new program to place first offenders in homes for supervision. He was one of the first to volunteer. Grandmother and Grandpa shared their home with the teenagers for more than six years. They slept four at a time in a large room with bunk beds and dressers provided by the state.

Grandmother agreed to let Grandpa do this work, although she worried about their own children. She worried that the teens would bring drugs into the house, or bad language, or disease, or all kind of things. She wanted Grandpa to be happy, so she worked along with him.

Meals were especially difficult. In the beginning of the program she would make a large salad of tomatoes, lettuce, cucumbers, green peppers, celery, onions and carrots and place it in the center of the table, followed by the meal. Each teen would get his turn as it was passed around. The first one said, "I can't eat the salad because I don't like carrots." The second said, "I don't like peppers, so I can't eat it." The third wouldn't like celery and so on around the table. The next time Grandmother made a salad, she placed the veggies in separate bowls and let them make their own.

Grandmother and Grandpa stuck with the program for about six years, and perhaps a hundred teenagers passed through their home. When the program ended, year after year the teens would write or come back, and thank Grandmother and Grandpa for helping them when they needed it most. Many of them never broke the law again. As far as Grandmother knew, their own children were never harmed by the teens, and learned how to love others who were different from themselves in some ways. Grandpa knew that they just needed more love and direction in their lives.

Sometimes it is hard to take a risk and help others when they need it. Jesus said there was once a man who was robbed, injured and left on the roadside by thieves. None of his friends stopped to help him. Finally a man stopped, bound up his wounds, took him to an inn, and paid the innkeeper to take care of him. Jesus told us to do this for others, not just our friends.

The Run-Away

"Mom," Grandmother's ten year old exclaimed as he burst through the door. "You remember that kid, John D., who lived with us last year? He's over on Robert's corner sitting on the sidewalk."

"Well, let's go over and see him," Grandmother answered as her son led her over to the corner on which John D. used to sit alone smoking cigarettes.

"Hi, John. . .you running away from some foster home?" Grandmother prompted him while inviting him to visit with them.

"No, I'm living with my grandmother two blocks away," answered John as he got up and started to follow Grandmother to the house.

Grandmother remembered that John was born in September, like herself, and liked to read, but mostly liked to run when things got too tough. I run at times, too, she thought. She remembered the time when Jesus was in the Garden of Gethsemane and asked His Father to remove the bitter cup of suffering, but then submitted to His Father's will. "Be it done to me according to Your Word." Jesus hung in for me because He loved me, and He loves John too.

So she said to John, "We got a new kid in the program yesterday, and as soon as he could, he asked when he was going to get an allowance. I thought, here we are, breaking our backs to keep this home together, the lights and water on, food on the table, clean sheets on the beds, and he wants to know when he is getting something more. I told him he had to work out a contract with my husband.

"When you came in, I was just thinking we are like that with God. He gives us a world to live in, air to breathe, food, light, warmth, love, all we need and more, and when we think of Him, if we think of Him

38

at all, the first thing we ask of Him is MORE when we should be thanking Him for the things we already have."

John looked at Grandmother, but did not say a word, so she continued, "I wrote this thanksgiving prayer,"

Dear Lord,

Can you explain to me why when I come home from work at night and find a new and nameless face before me, I always feel so repulsed at first? Every part of me rebels in self-defense and repugnance at this stranger invading my home. It is only after hours of just remaining in his presence and going about my duties as best I can that I begin to feel an ounce of human compassion for the boy. But eventually, Lord, something about him gets to me. Perhaps it is his infinite look of sadness, his obvious hunger for something more than the bread I offer him, or his hidden thirst for a word of acceptance from me, his homelessness with no place to lay his head; maybe it is the clothes he wears, his raggedy jeans, long hair, tennis shoes without laces. Soon, almost without my realizing it, he has moved into my reluctant heart and won a place there, and I know then that what happens to him after that matters to me. I look into his eyes and suddenly they are beautiful with a depth I had not noticed when I first came through the door. These foolish things, Lord, remind me of you.

"Is that really how you feel about us?" John asked.

"Yes, John, I really do. It's no different for me than for you."

The subject changed to a lighter note and John left after about an hour amidst laughter and good humor. Was he changed, Grandmother wondered? She didn't know the answer, but she knew she had changed because she had been honest with him about her feelings. Grandmother prayed that night. "When I come to your house, Jesus, I hope I remember to notice you live there. I hope I remember to thank you for being such a gracious host and for all your blessings. When you come to my house, Lord, I hope you won't be repulsed by my stingy, reluctant, unfeeling heart, but will stay long enough to change that heart into the kind we can offer together to our Father."

The Bible says that when you entertain a stranger, you may be entertaining angels. Jesus told us to love our enemies, because if we love our friends only, we are doing nothing special. He encouraged us to return good for evil and to bless those who curse us. How did Grandmother deal with her feelings?

The Bread of Christ

One of the teenagers who lived with Grandmother came to her one day and said, "I know how to make banana bread." So Grandmother bought the ingredients and turned the kitchen over to him while she visited a neighbor next door. When she returned and looked in the oven, she saw a bubbling-up glob of what was meant to become banana bread. After another half hour, she was sure it was not going to become bread. She asked the teen what he had put into it, going down the list of ingredients—bananas, eggs, vanilla, flour. "Flour!" he exclaimed. "Oh, my, I forgot the flour." So Grandmother said, "Never mind. We'll do it again tomorrow," which they did together and made a loaf of delicious banana bread.

There is one person in our lives we cannot live without if we want to become who we are meant to become. That person is Jesus Christ. Jesus is the ingredient that makes us whole. He said if we eat the Bread of Life we will have life in us and that life will increase. If we do not eat the Bread of Life, we will be incomplete, and will never know what we could become with Jesus helping us. Jesus said, "I am the vine and you are the branches." The branches must stay on the vine in order to bear fruit. We must remain in Jesus so that He can do the work God is calling us to do.

One day, Grandmother's daughter, Charlene, broke a branch from a tree. Grandmother scolded her, so she stuck it in the ground thinking it would grow. Grandmother explained to her that a branch cut off from a tree would not grow. Some branches do, however, sprout roots and grow again under the right circumstances. Some branches can be grafted onto other trees and become new trees with stronger flowers and fruit. Grandmother wondered about vines and if they could sprout roots and grow. She wondered about the words of Jesus.

"Remain in me, as I remain in you. Just as a branch cannot bear fruit on its own unless it remains on the vine, so neither can you unless you remain in me. I am the vine, you are the branches." John 15:4-5

Signs and Promises

Grandmother's daughter, Charlene, went on a cruise with friends. Grandmother went to the dock to see them leave. The ship went far out on the Atlantic Ocean until she could see it no more. She knew when it came into port there would be people waiting to meet them.

When Grandmother thought about Grandpa's death, she would sometimes cry. No one seemed to want to talk with her about it, as if it hadn't happened. She believed death was like the ship. When it left her sight, it came into heaven's port where God would meet him and he would begin a new journey into life. It was like being born again. A baby does not know what life is like in this world, but he wants to be born anyway. That is how Grandmother thought about death.

After Grandpa died, Charlene had a candlelight ceremony for family and friends who knew him. Everyone stood in a circle on the patio with a floating candle lit by Charlene and Jim. Then each person in turn said something good they remembered about Grandpa and put the candles in a bowl of water, where they made a bright circle of light. They prayed the Our Father, the prayer Jesus taught us, and everyone went inside where Grandmother served refreshments. It was Charlene's wish to have family rituals for his death so people would remember the good things Grandpa did, not the bad.

On the anniversary of Grandpa's death, Grandmother and Charlene bought a balloon filled with helium, tied a note and picture of Grandpa to it, and took it down to a little church on the Pacific Ocean in Kailua-Kona in Hawaii where Charlene lived. They let it go high up in the air, then went into the church and said a prayer.

Grandmother believes that Grandpa is busy in heaven helping St.

Joseph repair broken hearts on Earth and taking care of young people who need special care. That was when he was happiest on Earth.

Grandpa was not perfect, but when he failed to love, he would ask forgiveness of those he hurt and seek reconciliation with God. When young people got into trouble, he would look into their hearts and know they really did not want to do bad things. He knew God did not make junk. He had a rough time as a young boy and remembered what it felt like. He had a hard struggle in this life to believe that God loved him, but in the end he made peace with his family and God.

Jesus promised life everlasting to those who follow His commandment to love one another as He loved them. Even when there are problems and difficulties, Jesus told us He would be with us to help us.

The Kite Maker

Once upon a time, not so long ago, there was a small piece of cloth that lay in a basket among many other bits of cloth. One day, a father took the cloth and tore it into long, narrow pieces and tied them to a string to make a tail for his children's kite. The tail helped the kite to fly high in the sky. That made the children happy. Then, the wind died and the kite crashed to the ground, where it lay all alone.

In not too soon a time, a little girl came along, found the tail and took it home to her mother who sewed the pieces into a dress for her doll. The cloth was now happy because it was no longer alone. It remained on the doll for many years, until the little girl grew up and gave the dress to a vintage store. A lady came into the store one day, saw the cloth and said, "This will look beautiful in the quilt I am making for my bed." So the cloth now became part of a quilt, and was happy because it was part of something bigger than itself. The cloth lived happily among many other pieces of cloth on the quilt for many years and provided warmth for the lady as she grew older. When the quilt began to fade and no longer gave warmth to the lady, she gave it to a Second Hand Rose store where it lay on a shelf.

Now, it was at this time that an artist came into the store and saw the beautiful, faded quilt. She thought, "What lovely cloth paintings I could make from this old quilt," and she bought it. The piece of cloth, along with all the others, then became works of art, stuffed animals, quilt hangings and cloth paintings that decorated homes and made many people happy. The piece of cloth looked back on its life and thought about all the people it had made happy, how many lives it had touched, and how far it had traveled over the world. It was content.

God is a great artist who sits among Her human scraps of cloth as one of them. Her vision is to make them into one out of their differences. In the end She may string them all together like a tail at the end of a kite, and they will go sailing across the heavens, never to fall to earth, unless, of course, they want to.

The Piano

Great Grandmother was a Southern lady who believed in giving her children piano, voice and dance lessons. By the time she entered high school, Grandmother had completed almost ten years of piano and had achieved the status of a third grade pianist. Part of the problem was that she had a faulty muscle in her eye, which would not focus fast enough to look from the keys to the music, but most of it was because she did not have a gift for playing the piano. Her dearest wish as a child was to be part of a group, like a band or orchestra, not a soloist. Her mother had not recognized that need in her. Nevertheless, Grandmother was grateful to her mother. When she was older and alone when Grandfather died, she could read music and play the piano for her own enjoyment.

Grandmother had not always owned a piano. Providentially, someone she had not seen in over 40 years came back into her life at a high school reunion. Her friend had been part of a band in high school. He told her "Music is more than a way of communication. It makes you a part of something greater." Then she knew he understood. A band being out of the question, Grandmother followed her friend's suggestion that she buy an electronic keyboard. She searched in a warehouse until she found one that needed repair. The piano salesman told her it could be fixed and sold it to her on that condition. When the piano was delivered she turned it on and started to play. After twenty minutes it began to crackle just as the man had said.

One day she left the piano on for two hours and when she came home no sound came out of it. After another two hours cooling off, all the sound returned. She made a call to the piano repairman and he replaced two small electronic parts in the piano. Then she could play as long as she wished. Grandmother discovered that after years of typing on a computer her fingers were more limber and her playing improved, even though she had not played for over 40 years. The risk had been well worth taking, she reasoned.

Everyone plays a different instrument in the kingdom of God. The music is like an orchestra or band, and Jesus is the conductor. Many of the songs are love songs between our souls and God. Many also are songs all played together in praise of our Father. All are beautiful and in harmony with everyone else. Each person is happy to be part of something greater.

The Ballerina

After Grandmother's niece, Carrie Anne, came to live in Miami, she continued to take ballet lessons. At the very early age of one, after she learned to walk, she practiced dance steps from a coloring book her mother had bought. Her long journey from the dependence on the earth, mother and teacher, to that of freedom of expression as prima ballerina, was similar to the development of the butterfly.

The butterfly grows to be a beautiful creature from the darkness of the cocoon, to the freedom of flight into the sun. When Grandmother was taking a course in photography in college, she took a series of photographs of Carrie Anne as a ballerina. Carrie Anne had created a dance that told the story of becoming a butterfly, to symbolize the struggle of a little girl from her earliest days of putting up her long hair, to final triumph as a ballerina "on point." It symbolized a journey from childhood to adolescence to young womanhood. It represented the struggle the soul makes to leave the "cocoon" and discover the world, until finally reaching its heavenly home.

God never said it would be easy, Grandmother often reminded Carrie Anne, who succeeded in becoming a prima ballerina at long last, after many years of practice.

Peer Facilitator

When Carrie Anne was ten years old, Grandmother interviewed her for the camera course she was taking in college.

Q: What is a peer facilitator?

A: Someone who is a friendly helper, a very careful listener, and cares about her peers.

Q: How did you become a peer facilitator?

A: My fourth grade teacher mentioned some children he felt would be good peer facilitators, and I was one of them. There were eight children chosen.

Q: What school did you attend?

A: Fruitville Elementary (outside of Sarasota, Florida)

Q: What do you think about your school?

A: They don't let you do what you want to do, but they're not as strict and mean as some.

Q: Are you part of a gifted program?

A: No, this is a school for normal kids.

Q: What kind of training did you receive in order to become a peer facilitator?

A: The school counselor teaches you what she knows. You get a green booklet of about twenty pages. You fill out some papers about what you feel, how you enjoy helping others. They ask you if you want to do it and if they think you have the personality, they ask you to become a peer facilitator.

Q: What else did you have to do?

A: I read the chapters and did the activities. I practiced careful listening techniques. They held meetings twice a week and we practiced the exercises and activities. Sometimes we missed classroom studies and had to work harder on weekends and evenings to catch up.

Q: Please describe a typical situation in which you counseled one of your peers. Do know what peer means?

A: No.

Grandmother explained to Carrie Anne the meaning of the word "peer." It means someone like yourself—a student your age, or in my case, an adult or person my age. Carrie Anne continued: I started out in Ms. B's class. I counseled a child named Tanya who had trouble smiling. She did not have a physical problem; it was emotional. She did not participate with the other children and was very, very shy and hurt in some ways. If someone said hi, she didn't say hello back. She didn't even smile. I counseled her and in the first three weeks she improved a great deal. I sat down with her every day for one-half hour and talked with her. "Tanya, has someone been mean to you?" She didn't answer. Sometimes she would say no. "Tanya, I want to be your friend." And one day she said, "You do?" I said yes. Every day I came back; now, Tanya smiles and plays with the other children. That was my first case.

Q: Is there anyone else you have helped?

A: Yes, one other; me.

Q: How do you feel about yourself as a peer facilitator?

A: I felt I was able to use the careful listening technique a lot. That is the most important one. Inside, it made me feel warm and glowing, like the feeling you get at Christmas.

Q: How do your peers accept you as a peer facilitator?

A: Some of my classmates make fun of me, but a few understand. Teresa, Jessica and Nicholas understand. They encourage me. I have helped Nicholas, but not the others. Nicholas gets made fun of and cries, but when I ask if I can help, he says to leave him alone. But I come back and ask again. He says, "Everybody makes fun of me."

Q: Do you see this as something Jesus would want you to do?

A: (Eyes light up) Yes.

Q: When you grow up, do you think you will continue to be a peer facilitator?

A: I believe if I were working in an office and a secretary felt down—maybe her boyfriend had left her—I would definitely help. I might want to start a group that would become part of every school system.

Q: If you were in a program for gifted children, do you think you would have an opportunity to be a peer facilitator?

A: Yes, gifted children have a lot of problems. They don't seem to know how to handle it if someone tells them they are ugly or something.

Grandmother read the interview with her niece again. She had not read it for a long time. Her niece was now 18. Grandmother thought to herself, Carrie Anne is still a careful listener and helps those who need her. Grandmother thought it would be wonderful if everyone could learn how to be a "careful listener." The world would get better overnight.

Talents

Grandmother, as you know by now, loved to spend money. Her children always told her she couldn't manage money. Nevertheless, over the years she did manage, often on one salary, and there were always plenty of presents at Christmas, even when she told her children there would not be any "this year." When she retired, Grandmother lived on Social Security and pensions from her work (for over 45 years), and she had to learn how to live on a budget. Then she learned how to make money without having a lot. It happened this way:

One day the telephone company sent Grandmother a letter with a check for $40.00. Her first thought was to rush to the bank and deposit it. Instead, she thought about it. Once before she had received a check from them, cashed it, and changed telephone carriers. The next year another carrier sent her a check to change companies, so she changed again to another company. Now, after another year passed, a new company called and offered her a new deal. This time she called her company and told them the story (which by now they had heard from other customers as well). Her present company told her not to cash the check and they would send her a certificate that would earn money, and at the end of the year she could use it on her phone bill. So, Grandmother stayed with her carrier, earned money and forgot the whole thing. The next year when a new company sent her another check to change, she remembered the certificate and called her now steady company. They told her it had increased in value to $100.00. She cashed it in for three months worth of telephone bills. Grandmother hoped no one would send her any more checks because she promised her carrier to stay with them if they kept her rate low. That was how Grandmother earned money she did not earn.

In the kingdom of God, everyone will be able to use talents and gifts to please God. In this life we may do all we can to increase the gifts and talents God gives us in order to know, love and serve God and others. If we truly love God, we will want to use all his gifts well. He has given us a mind and a heart to use, so we must use them as best we can.

On Lava Mountain

The lava rock crunched beneath Grandmother's feet, snapped, crackled and popped as she made her way to the newest lava flow on Kilauea crater in Hawaii. She learned from the guide the rock was just three to four weeks hardened, which made it light and porous, and accounted for the sound. As she grew closer she felt the heat seep out between the same fissures that, coming back after sunset, would reveal red-hot flowing lava. Before and behind her in a single line, people were inching their way over the surface like a line of ants approaching a morsel of food. As Grandmother stepped nearer to the flow she saw the fiery red lava oozing out of the hardening surface, like honey oozing out of a bottle. The lava looked like wave after wave of black tar as it found an opening, hardened in the cool air and surfaced in a new place.

The park official told the visitors the flow was traveling so fast down the mountain into the Pacific Ocean, off the coast of Hawaii, it might trap the people. They would have to begin now to make their way the one-quarter mile back before dark. As the sun was setting, Grandmother looked back and saw a fiery trail of lava as it surfaced in the cracks all the way down the mountain. The sight of the red-hot lava made Grandmother unsteady as she carefully wound her way down the mountain. At one point she felt a hand reach out for hers. A young Japanese athlete grabbed her hand and steadied her the rest of the way down. At the bottom Grandmother thanked the strong young girl and gave her a hug. Just behind, her daughter was having her own struggle with camera gear, flashlight, jackets and other paraphernalia they had brought with them.

Grandmother reflected on her experience. It reminded her of the many sermons she had heard in the past on "hell." She realized her own purification was being accomplished through God's love and that this love is hotter than all the "fires of hell." She knew God would steady her and bring her safely "down the mountain" of life.

The Carpenter

After Grandpa died, Grandmother lived in a townhouse in Davie, Florida. One day she decided to have a carpenter rebuild her stairway to the loft to make it stronger. Everyone in Florida took precautions to secure their homes from the threat of hurricanes.

She watched the carpenter move a small plastic box with two button-sized lights over the wall. Suddenly, the green light turned off and the red light flashed. "When the light changes from green to red," he explained to the bewildered grandmother, "it means there is a stud in the wall and I can nail the board at that point to make it secure."

The carpenter had been rounding off corners, filing, sanding, filling, staining and varnishing each step to fit every other step. As the staircase wound its way to the loft above, the skylights shone bluer than blue and the sun poured its golden rays into the house to nourish the green, hanging plants below.

God's kingdom is like a carpenter who searches and finds strong beams to support his house. When he finds a beam, he nails other boards to the beam until he forms a structure. When the structure is strong he can lay the more delicate materials to it until he builds a room or a flight of stairs, and the house can withstand the forces of nature, which a family can live in.

When God builds His Church, Grandmother thought, He must find people who can withstand the pressure of the elements or the world like the house. They must stand firm and hold others up by their faith that comes from God. If they are nailed to the I-beam, which is Christ, the structure or the Church will be strong enough to support the people. Then the children of the kingdom can come to the Church and know His care and love and live in God's house because they know the structure is strong and will not break.

"In my Father's house are many mansions."

*W*heels

One day Nicholas's dad took him on a merry-go-round with horses that go up and down in rhythm with the music. When the music stopped, his dad lifted him from the horse and onto the ground. The wheels in Nicholas's head were still whirring with the last few circles of the merry-go-round, but when it stopped he bent over and looked underneath to see what made it go around.

When Nicholas was under a year old, his Grandmother would take him in his stroller for a walk around the block and point out flowers, trees and birds. But Nicholas only wanted to watch the wheels on his stroller go around, so he kept his head bent down to watch them turn.

Nicholas loved trains, trucks, steering wheels, fire engines, all types of construction toys, and wanted to know how they worked. Sometimes he would take them apart to find out. Nicholas had been watching the "There Goes a Spaceship" video. He took a spaceman from his Burger King kid's lunch and pretended to be a spaceman. He told Grandmother to be "Nicholas." When "Nicholas" asked to go up in the spaceship, the astronaut (Nicholas) answered, "Sorry, there is no room in the spaceship." Grandmother thought she had heard those words before. Then she remembered she had read Nicholas the story of the Nativity and guessed Nicholas had learned those words from the story. She was sure of it when he said, "But I'll go look if I can find some space for you." The astronaut went off to look for some space and when he came back he said, "Yes, there's some space here.

All aboard. Grandmother was happy that Nicholas had rewritten the story to make some space for "Nicholas."

God is a great storyteller. He has a space for all His children. He will bring them close to Him and explain how the wheels in heaven work. Then he will let the children ride on the heavenly trucks, fire engines and trains as long as they like. They will then understand how everything works and won't have to look underneath at earth to try to figure it all out.

Daddy

When Nicholas was three years old, Grandmother asked him "Who made you?"

"Daddy made me," Nicholas replied. "He made my arms and head..." and he put his hands on his little chest indicating the rest of his body.

"Did Mommy make you too?" Grandmother hopefully asked.

"No," he answered without hesitation.

So Grandmother started to say, "God made you," but decided that "Daddy" would do. She told Nicholas "Daddy" was God's name too. Grandmother thought someday Nicholas will call God "God," but now he might think it rather odd to know someone made him he can't see; so isn't it better, she reasoned, to call God "Daddy?"

When she told this story to her daughter-in-law, however, Tina was not too happy about it, so she began to tell Nicholas a few more "facts of life." Now Nicholas says Daddy and Mommy made him and also Tiffany, Dougy, Grandmother and the dog and cat.

Three is not a very good age to learn about sex. Grandmother remembered when she tried to tell her own daughter about the birds and the bees. Charlene, then four years old, told Grandmother she was going to have a baby because she swallowed a seed. Grandmother told her not to worry, it was an accident. Charlene replied, "No, Mama, I did it on purpose."

St. Joseph was the foster-father of Jesus, which means that God gave him the task of being a "Daddy" to Jesus while He lived on the earth. We all need caretakers in our lives, people who take care of us while our parents work or are not available. We love, respect and obey our caretakers just as if they were our own mothers and fathers. St. Joseph took good care of Jesus, taught Him prayers, how to be a carpenter and took him to church. Jesus obeyed Mary and Joseph because it was God's will. Even after he stayed behind in the temple, he returned to Nazareth and obeyed them. Jesus lived at home until he was 30 years old, and even after St. Joseph died, He remained at home and helped His mother. This was a special time for both of them, just as it is for children who live at home until they are ready to enter the world.

When Jesus spoke of His Father, he called him lovingly "Abba" which is translated "Daddy," someone with whom He was familiar. When we pray to God, we can think of Him as both a mother and a father. Jesus once spoke of Himself as a mother who wanted to comfort her children. "Jerusalem, Jerusalem, I would have gathered you as a hen gathers her chicks under her wings..." St. Therese said to be boldly confident in the arms of your Father, like a child who loves and trusts his Father enough to keep him safe from harm.

True Friends

Grandmother believed Jesus was the best friend she ever had. He was always there when she needed to talk with Him, was her daily companion in all her work and activities, rejoiced with her when she was glad, and comforted her when she was sad. When she needed a little extra love or a hug, He managed to find someone to send into her life to give it.

It had not always seemed to Grandmother to be that way. She remembered her own mother was sick with tuberculosis and not physically available to her as a child. Her father was too busy making a living, and anyway, hugging and kissing were not something all people did in those days, even when they were well. When Grandmother married Grandfather she did not follow the same tradition, but instead made sure the kids got lots of affection.

One day Grandmother looked into the big, brown, round eyes of Nicholas and touched his curly blond head. Just for a moment she felt as if her hands were the hands of Mary, and Jesus was standing there smiling up at her. At that moment Grandmother understood how precious life is, how precious the body of Christ. She understood Jesus was present in herself, her children, and her grandchildren in a very special way, and she hoped when she hugged them or touched them they would experience her love and respect for them.

Grandmother thought what a terrible thing it is to destroy a life, which God made, or hurt a child made in His image and likeness. She prayed for those who would knowingly or unknowingly hurt one of God's little ones. One day in church she looked around her and noticed the statues had been replaced, it seemed, by the people of God. It was as if they came down from their stands and began to move into the aisles and shake hands with everyone and give them a hug or a kiss of peace. She thought it took thousands of years, people and a council to make the change, but it was the right thing to do.

Passing down the aisle after church, she looked over and found a wall statue. It was a trilogy of Mary holding a Rosary, Jesus holding a lamb, and St. Joseph holding an anvil. Grandmother thought of her hand on the curly head of Nicholas and the smile on his face. It was at that moment she remembered Nicholas had been holding a wooden hammer resembling Joseph's.

Grandmother's chosen granddaughter, Tiffany, was only four years old when she met her, but Tiffany was spunky and seemed to know her own worth. Grandpa was retired and very sick with cancer. He had picked setting the table and other chores around the house as his contribution to the family. When the little bundle of energy, Tiffany, arrived for dinner one evening, she decided to help Grandmother set the table. Grandpa looked at her, stuck out his tongue in jest and said, "That's my job." Tiffany returned the gesture, continuing to set the table.

At the marriage of her mother to Grandmother's son, Tiffany gave Grandmother a long, wet kiss on the lips because she thought she was getting married as well.

As a child, Grandmother was not allowed to speak when grownups were talking, or enter into adult conversations. Grandmother felt as a child her affection had been repressed, and she was not able to so demonstrably and spontaneously show affection the way Tiffany could. Later Grandmother learned Tiffany was in need of being held and hugged as much as Nicholas and needed this assurance of Grandmother's affection. She wished her parents had been affectionate with her, so she began to hug Tiffany too.

One day Grandmother tried to explain St. Joseph's relationship to Jesus, thinking it would help her accept her new stepfather. She told Tiffany that God loved her and put people on earth to show his love. She simply replied, "I love myself." Grandmother thought if everyone could learn to love others as themselves, there would be far fewer problems in the world.

Tiffany was becoming a beautiful young lady now, who loved her brother, Nicholas, very much. She thought he was smart beyond his age. She tried to teach Nicholas the things he needed to know. She taught him his ABC's, numbers, colors and shapes by the time he was three. Sometimes Nicholas tired of school and then Grandmother had to help Tiffany learn to make it fun in short intervals. That was easy for Grandmother because she enjoyed teaching her own students in third grade for many years. Tiffany, however, found it spoiled her efforts, although Nicholas was happy to go back to his wheels.

Sisters

When Grandmother was between the ages of eighteen and twenty, she led her sister down the lonely path of atheism, because her friends thought they were atheists and she thought they knew better than she.

When she was 23, God gave her the gift of faith. Then Grandmother remembered the Lord's words with fear. "If you lead one of these little ones astray, it were better for you had you never been born…"

Twenty years later her sister came to see Grandmother and they prayed together. After a moment Grandmother asked her sister's forgiveness for her transgression. Her sister, Marilyn, remained quiet while tears of joy fell down her cheeks. Grandmother saw her sister's faith and confidence in her restored before her eyes. She felt all the years of bitterness fall away, and since her sister had long since become a Christian, Grandmother knew God had forgiven them for their childhood ignorance of His love.

Grandmother and her sister sometimes discussed some of the differences in their faith. For example, Grandmother would explain her deep love for Mary, the mother of Jesus. Every time she would say "Mary," Marilyn would say "Jesus." Many people did not have an understanding of Grandmother's love for Mary, thinking she was dishonoring Jesus as Lord by honoring his mother. On the way home, Grandmother realized Marilyn had proved the point she had been making.

Church doctors tell us that Mary never wanted to receive any glory for herself, nor wanted to take any away from her Son. Her only wish was to see Jesus grow in our souls in wisdom and in grace before God the Father. She is mother of the head, Jesus, and mother of the body, the Church. She is mother of both. How can one separate the head from the body, Grandmother thought?

Theologians tell us when we say "Mary" Mary says "Jesus," and that is exactly what Grandmother's sister did. So when she got home, she called her on the phone and told her, "Marilyn, you are the best example of what I was trying to explain to you because every time I said "Mary," you said "Jesus," and that is what Mary does. She thought Mary must really love Marilyn because she is just like her.

If we listen carefully to those who say they believe differently from us, we often find they think the same way we do. Arguing really is of no help. If we show them God's love, He will do the rest. That is how Grandmother received the gift of faith when she was 23, by living with a Christian family who showed her God's love.

Behold Your Mother

Grandmother received a letter from her son in the Navy for Mother's Day. His ship, the U.S.S. Nimitz, had been deployed in the Persian Gulf during the 1980 crisis in Lebanon, and he was homesick. Grandmother often read the letter because it made her think of Mary, the mother of Jesus, and all she suffered to be His mother and now the mother of the Body of Christ. Her son wrote:

"I saw vividly someone always there. Someone who kept faith in someone I felt couldn't exist. Someone who spoke of encouragement while we all looked through a haze of confusion; who worked all her life to support a family, whether it was her mother's or her own. Someone who believed with all that exists within her in a team called a family. Someone who raised me with morals that to this day keep me from doing things I might otherwise be doing. I can't think of one instance when she wasn't there for me, even when I didn't want her. One who sensed my problems and troubles, no matter how hard I tried to keep them hidden. Our minds could touch one another's.

Through all the diaper changing, the grocery shopping, dinners, Christmases, Thanksgivings and birthdays, she tried and succeeded far beyond what I could ever understand. So, in my sleep, I discover the one who was the rock, who was stronger than any force of evil. She said no, wouldn't stand to see this family destroyed.

I love you, Mom. May we always be reminded of the love you've given us, not just on Mother's Day."

While waiting for her car to be serviced, Grandmother watched a mother with a 14-month-old baby. The mother was totally devoted to the baby's every need. When it cried, she comforted it; when it laughed, she sang to it; her total strength and attention was given to the baby, centered around his dependence on her. Grandmother thought if only we could be like this with God. He would fulfill our every wish provided it was for our good. All we would have to do is love Him, cry out when we were in need; laugh, enjoy, or hurt and know He cares. Who can imagine a more devoted mother than Mary must have been, one who desired to see her Son grow in strength, wisdom and understanding.

Mary was human like us. Both she and St. Joseph knew what it was to study, work and pray. She struggled with everyday tasks like spinning cloth to make clothing, cooking, cleaning, and all without modern conveniences such as we have.

Just before Jesus died, He looked down and saw his mother and St. John, the one apostle who did not abandon Him. He said to John, "Son, behold your mother," and to His mother, "Woman, behold your son." By these words He gave His mother over to the care of John who took her into his home. She also took care of St. John and became our mother as well. She takes care of us the same way she did for Jesus. Her only concern is to see that Jesus grows in wisdom, strength and understanding in each one of her children. She is Our Mother of Perpetual Help, which means she will always help us to know, love and serve God in this world and live with Him forever in His kingdom.

"When Jesus saw his mother and the disciple there whom he loved, he said to his mother, 'Woman, behold, your son.' Then he said to the disciple, 'Behold, your mother.' And from that hour the disciple took her into his home." John 19:26-27

Kyra's Christmas Gift

Once upon a time, not so long ago, there was a little girl named Kyra who lived in a beautiful neighborhood called Victoria Park in Fort Lauderdale, Florida. There were many children living in her neighborhood who played with Kyra and were her friends. When she was one year old, Grandmother had a Christmas party for all the grandchildren and invited Kyra, her mother Melissa, and other grandmother, Donna, to the party, along with other friends.

Grandmother bought a rag doll for Kyra, put it in a fancy box, wrapped it in Christmas paper, tied it with ribbon, and gave it to Kyra at the party. When she opened her gift, Kyra picked up the doll and threw it across the room as far as her little arms could throw it. Everyone was stunned and a little embarrassed, but Kyra sat down on the floor, climbed into the box and looked up with a contented smile. Then everyone started laughing and Grandmother said, "See, kids like the boxes to play with, not the toys."

Kyra was trying to tell us in her own way what Christmas is all about. Christmas is the time when Jesus came to be our first present. When Kyra climbed into the box she was telling us a baby is our best Christmas present. Some come wrapped up in black, some brown, some red, some beige, some white, but God equally loves all.

Messes

"Clean up your room, it's a mess," Nicholas often heard from grownups. But he had a different idea. Nicholas told Grandmother he liked to make a mess.

Grandmother thought about that for a while. Her thoughts went something like this. God must like a mess too. Every year the leaves fall off the trees in the north and people have to rake them. Snow falls on the ground and is piled high in the streets and sidewalks and people have to plow through them. Rivers overflow, rain comes down on picnics, clouds bounce around in the blue sky, weeds and flowers grow side by side, insects eat the flower seeds or spoil the flowers themselves, and on and on she counted the messes. She was stuck for an answer.

Then Grandmother remembered the spring up North when she was a young girl. She remembered the violets in the snow, the blossoms on the trees, the buds, new leaves, baby peeps, rabbits, Easter eggs, resurrection, joy. She remembered Nicholas was only three, and since she felt better now after her minute meditation, she said "OK. Nicholas, you can make a mess now, but at the end of the day, please help me clean up the mess."

"No talk, Gamma," said Nicholas busy making his mess.

Grandmothers see miracles where others see only messes.

In the kingdom of God we have to believe and trust God loved us so much He sent His own Son to live, suffer and die for us to clean up the mess of original sin. He gives us all the grace we need and helps us in cleaning up our own messes as well. When Jesus rose from the dead He told us He would be with us always, to the end of the world.

The Yarn Doll

Grandmother made her daughter a small yarn doll just the way her own grandmother made them when she was a little girl. She took pink yarn, wound it around her hand, tied it in the middle and cut it into even lengths. Next, she took a piece of yarn and tied a bundle to make the head. She divided it between head and body and placed pieces of tied yarn in the center for arms. Finally, she tied the waist to make a body, decorated it with lace and ribbons and gave it to Charlene.

Charlene kept the yarn doll among her boxes of small remembrances for many years until she was graduated from college. The she moved to Colorado to work. Since she was now grown, Charlene felt she could part with her doll, so when she was ready to leave Colorado she had a garage sale. She put a sign on her doll for one dollar because it was still in good condition. No one bought her doll, so she reclaimed it and moved to San Francisco.

While in San Francisco, Charlene, now a fine married lady, had another garage sale where she parted with more of her small remembrances, and once more her yarn doll. She put a tag on it for fifty cents because now it had a small tear in the lace. No one bought it. Then she moved with her husband to Hawaii.

In Hawaii, Charlene had a sidewalk sale and placed her small doll on a table with a tag, which said 25 cents, because now it was slightly faded and had a small tear in the lace.

No one bought her doll.

Then Charlene had a bright idea. She offered her doll to the hospice where she worked for their charity sale. The sign on it said

10 cents because it was slightly faded, had a small tear on the lace, and the body was worn.

No one bought her doll.

Then she gave her doll to the AIDS society for their sale and they kept the 10 cents sign on it. When she returned later that day she found her doll still there on the table since no one had bought it. Charlene looked at it sadly and said to herself, "Well, it must be that I am supposed to keep my doll," and she purchased it back for 10 cents and brought it home.

When Charlene reluctantly told her mother the story, thinking she would be hurt, Grandmother told her "Please send the doll back to me so I can keep it and someday tell your daughter about the little yarn doll that went halfway around the world and came home to stay."

In the kingdom of God, the Lord will mend all our tears, give us non-faded clothes to wear and make us new again. Then we can travel all over the universe with Him and He will never want to leave us. He will never, ever sell us in a garage sale no matter how good the cause. We will be permanently His forever and ever.

Grandmother's Loft

Nicholas liked to play in the loft at his Grandmother's house. He would climb up a flight of stairs to the top floor where he could play in two dollhouses and a country store. He liked to play with the Shirley Temple Little Princess doll with a crown on her head and a white stole on her shoulders, holding a scepter in her hand.

Nicholas took the crown, stole and scepter from Shirley, put the crown on his head, the stole over his shoulders and the scepter in his hand. With his curly, blond hair, he looked like a stand-in for Shirley.

Nicholas would play in the dollhouses too. He would cook, make tea for Grandmother and serve Shirley lunch. Then he bought food from the country store and delivered it to the children he knew did not have food after the hurricanes in South Florida.

In the heavenly loft, Jesus will give all His brothers and sisters crowns, scepters and white stoles trimmed in gold. When he finds them faithful over a few things, He will let them rule over many and help others the way a good prince or princess would do.

The Birds

As Grandmother sat under the Australian pines at St. David Church, she listened to the incessant chirping of the birds overhead. Over the years they had become tame as they waited impatiently for the people to leave the picnic grounds after church. Then they would swoop down out of the tree branches—left somewhat bare by Florida's hurricane winds—pick up scraps of donuts or pancakes in their beaks and fly off to devour their prize. In such surroundings it was easy for Grandmother to understand how God provided for the birds. They did not have to worry about their food, but just had to wait for the people to inadvertently provide it by their pancake breakfasts and donut ministry.

Even if the birds didn't get pancakes every Sunday, God provided them with seeds, berries and feathers to keep warm, so they did not have to worry, but could just chirp away at praising God by being themselves.

Perhaps that is really what God enjoys most in His kingdom, and why He doesn't want us to worry too much about the details. In God's kingdom, people will have everything they need to make them happy, so they can spend all their time praising God and making Him loved on earth as in Heaven.

The Caretaker

"And God said, 'Let the water teem with living creatures, and let the birds fly above the earth across the expanse of the sky.'" Genesis 1: 20

Grandmother had been stewing all day over her finances. She knew it was her fault she was in debt, but she worried how she would pay it. At the same time, she knew she would have to trust God to help her. She prayed that morning for help as she often prayed for her daily bread.

Just then she heard a flutter outside in her garden. She walked to the sliding glass door and watched a dove perching on the feeder, busily picking up seeds in its beak. Soon she saw a blue jay dive headfirst into the birdbath she had fashioned out of clay, flutter its wings, dip its body in the cool water and serenely preen its feathers. The dove flew away as Grandmother watched, while a calm settled over her. A wren flew over to replace the dove, soon to be followed by a black bird, a robin and a yellow-throated Baltimore oriole. All afternoon she returned to the glass door to watch the birds bathe and feed themselves.

Sometimes the birds did not behave at all well. The blue jays wasted the food, eating only what they liked, and tossed the rest to the ground. The black birds squawked and tried to push the blue jays from the ledge. The doves, on the other hand, stayed on the ground and ate whatever they found there, not caring to join in the squabble, it seemed. Occasionally, a wren, not finding a bird perched on the ledge, would come down and enjoy a quiet feast. Even the doves, however, would fight among themselves over the food from time to time. How like children they are, Grandmother thought.

As she gazed over the top of the climbing rosebush with its fiery coral blossoms, she grew very quiet and contemplative. Inside she began to hear the words of a very close friend: "Why do you worry about what you will eat or what you will wear? I know you need these things. Do I not provide for the birds of the air? Your Father knows you have need of such things. Look at the flowers in your garden. They neither spin nor sew, yet no one is clothed as they are."

Grandmother walked slowly away from the door, confident that no matter what would happen, as long as she was able, she would continue to provide birdseed and fill the birdbath with water for her little winged messengers.

$\mathcal{P}$lans

When a woman is young, life spreads out before her like a quilt, colorful, full of patterns and ideas. Without experience to hold her back, she can make all kinds of plans for the future and life is beautiful, exciting and seems as if it will go on forever.

As she grows older and has some experience behind her, she finds it hard to just let go, relax and take it one day at a time. She has always had children to care for, or a job, or someone waiting for her to come home. She seldom has time to make plans and dream of the future. It seems to her then that something always has to be accomplished before she can rest. Even after children are grown and leave home, or someone she loves dies and she is left alone, she still feels she has to rush home to prepare dinner or take care of the house, or worry about her grandchildren or her own children and wonder how they are doing with their lives.

But Jesus said not to worry about the cares of tomorrow. Today there is enough to worry about. Take it one day at a time.

Wouldn't it be nice if a woman could just sit down beside Jesus in her home and he would discuss His plans for her future and listen to hers? Perhaps he would begin by giving her a hug and then take her hand in his and tell her how beautiful she is and how much he loves her. He does, you know.

In the kingdom of heaven, God will meet each one of his children face to face, sit with them, tell them all of His plans for them, listen to theirs, give them a hug and a kiss of peace, and they will never have to worry again.

The Dump Truck

When Nicholas visited Grandmother, he loved to watch the garbage truck dump the trash into its belly on trash day. He would wait by the window until the truck arrived in front of the dumpster. When the driver backed up the truck, Nicholas listened to the "beep" as the driver headed toward him waving and blowing his horn.

Nicholas loved trucks and all vehicles with wheels, so Grandmother bought him an entire set of "There Goes a Truck, Fire Engine, Train and Spaceship," and other videos of real-life people working in the world, which he prefers to cartoons.

One day Grandmother decided there might be a better way to dump the trash in her life instead of always burdening others with it. Of course, she thought, sometimes it helps to sort it out, clarify it, organize it, file it and dispose of some of it, but clearly some is also recyclable into beautiful creations, such as stories.

God has given us a wonderful vehicle for dumping garbage, called reconciliation. When we are sorry, we can ask God's and the other person's forgiveness. We can often get to the bottom of the trash heap and find the root cause of the problem. Then we can recycle what we discover into useful information for our growth in love. Talking with the right person about our problems is half the battle.

Grandpa used to say to us, "It is good never to let the sun go down on your anger."

Music, Music, Music

Grandmother received a CD player for Christmas from her children. She started driving around to garage sales collecting "oldies" for 50 cents each because she wanted to hear her old favorites again. The music she liked was from the 30s and 40s, like Bessie Smith, Billie Holiday, Irish minstrels, blues, jazz, love songs, and some classical music.

One Saturday she walked into a music store and went to the oldies section to look for her favorites. She only found music from the 60s, and that was not oldie enough for her. Finally, the saleslady showed her some old oldies in another section, so she bought some. She drove home, put the discs in her CD player and her little townhouse started rocking with the music of her choice.

When the grandchildren came to see her, they wanted to know where all that old music came from and why didn't she get some new music, but Grandmother only smiled and said, "Why not try something new?"

As Grandmother listened to her music, she began to think about the music in heaven and what it must be like. She imagined the kingdom of heaven as an orchestra. There were an infinite variety of musical instruments for the people to play. All the instruments have been perfectly tuned by Mary and her helper angels; and when the orchestra is playing, each instrument harmonizes with every other instrument. The song is Jesus singing to his Father. There are deep voices; pure, sweet melodies; light, delicate ones; strong, beating ones; new and old voices, all playing the music of heaven.

Mary and her helpers are busy finely tuning the hearts of the children of God on earth. There are broken hearts that must be mended, lonely hearts to be loved and hearts missing a beat that must be made whole again so they can join the orchestra. From their home in heaven, St. Joseph, along with St. Nicholas and other helper saints, perform this work of love.

Jesus wants to play a song of love on our hearts. If our heart is broken, we may ask Him to fix it. If we are lonely, we may ask Jesus to come into our heart. If our heart needs a little tuning, we may ask Mary, His mother, or another saint to gently tune it; and if we are really bent out of shape, Jesus may apply a little force.

Then listen to the music, music, music.

Going into the Closet

When Grandmother retired from her administrative assistant job, she found she had a lot of time on her hands. She soon discovered how to become a professional "closet re-doer."

This was a hazardous task, as everyone soon found out. When she began to organize her closets, they were in for a surprise. First, she called her children and arranged for them to pick up their belongings. Out came boxes of small remembrances: trophies, golf clubs, baseball gloves, truck tires, wheels, records, tapes, hats, clothes, photo albums, dollhouses, books, shoes and school papers. Reluctant to make room in their own closets, the boxes remained in the hallway for a long time, waiting for the children to come get them. But Grandmother persevered and walked around the boxes for months, until finally they came for them.

Grandmother's daughter Charlene was the first one to come all the way from Hawaii where she lived. Charlene was blonde, tall, outgoing and beautiful in body and spirit. When Grandmother's friend met her as a child, he said, "She is the outgoing one."

The boxes brought out many memories for Charlene. She remembered when they were teenagers, she and her brother Jim wanted to see "Saturday Night Fever" and Grandmother said no. Later, Charlene wanted to see the "Exorcist" and Grandmother said no again, but looked in the paper to see what PG (Parental Guidance) movies were playing at the local theater. She found one entitled "Lies My Father Taught Me" and took them to see it. Much to her surprise there were nude scenes in the movie and Grandmother did not understand how they could give it a PG rating. When they left the theater, no one said anything, but when picking up her boxes those many years later, Charlene laughed and said, "You let us see that movie and wouldn't let us see 'Saturday Night Fever'." By then both of them had seen it and didn't understand why all the fuss. Grandmother decided you couldn't always depend on movie ratings.

Charlene had also asked to buy the book "The Exorcist" when it came out, and said at 13, "I'll put it in the closet and read it when I am 18." The book stayed there for many years and no one read it. She also hid a picture and a miniature bottle of vodka, one of several that made its way into a pre-teen party. No too long after the boys spiked the punch, the girls started crying—from the vodka, no doubt—and a happy party turned sour. Apparently, they had been having some pre-teen boyfriend problems and became overly emotional with the vodka. Grandmother, who had been chaperoning the party from the next room, at her daughter's request, didn't know about the vodka. She wondered why all the girls were crying. Charlene told her later that night the girls had not known about the punch. Yes, the boxes held many memories for Charlene.

Then it was Jim's turn. He had to pile his car high with speakers, tires, tapes, Navy gear, sports equipment, books and even a small metal box he kept his first girlfriend's pigtail in that she had given him when he went into the Navy.

Finally, the boxes were gone. Grandmother then took a trip to Home Depot and discovered there are shelves for just about anything your heart could desire. Trying to find the perfect shelf for each group of items became the challenge. There were shelves for sweaters, shoes, hats; corner shelves, hanging shelves, shelves to store ribbons and boxes; Christmas-ball boxes, hooks for scarves; shelves for towels, sports equipment and even underwear. Then there were decisions about space (filling up each inch was the goal), how to store heavy items and how to put it all together in which closet. It was a complex project indeed. Now that Grandmother was accomplished at going into the closet and bringing out all her memories, she had to sort the rest of the items and place them neatly on shelves. It took a long time, but finally it was accomplished.

Jesus said in the end God would separate the ones who loved from the ones who failed to love. Sometimes it is hard to understand why there is evil in the world alongside the good, but Jesus said if you pull up the weeds, the good seed or flowers might be uprooted as well. It is best to let them grow side by side until the end. That is why we pray for those who do evil, and let God do His job.

"...If you pull up the weeds you might uproot the wheat along with them. Let them grow together until harvest; then at harvest time I will say to the harvesters, 'First collect the weeds and tie them in bundles for burning; but gather the wheat into my barn'" *Matthew13:29-30*

Treasure

On a cool Sunday morning in Florida, Grandmother went to the post office next to St. David's Church. She went inside the post office, bought some stamps from the machine and mailed her letters. Then she went to the picnic area outside the church where she often waited for the Mass to begin, arriving early for a cup of coffee and a donut. She enjoyed being under the trees with the people's voices surrounding her, the birds singing and the cool air circling around her body. On Sunday, Grandmother always put on a little makeup because she was going to meet Jesus in the Eucharist, as food for her body and soul. She liked to see the people enjoying themselves first. When she held the hand of the one next to her at the Our Father, she remembered the good feeling of being with them in the open air, like Jesus when He first taught the prayer to his disciples.

This morning, a young boy was intently walking around the area searching for bright, shiny coins that people had unwittingly dropped under the tables. As his eye caught one, he would reach down, pick it up and drop it in his pocket. As he walked on, Grandmother could see a glint of triumph in his eyes, a sense of achievement in having outsmarted some careless grownups!

"Do not store up for yourselves treasures on earth, where moth and decay destroy, and thieves break in and steal. But store up treasures in Heaven, where neither moth nor decay destroys, nor thieves break in and steal. For where your treasure is, there also will your heart be. Matthew 6:9-21

86

The Baker

"In a bakery," the man explained to Grandmother, "your tools lie all around you, and when you use one, you drop it on the bench and pick up another one. At the end of the day the dishwasher gathers all of your tools, washes them and returns them to the bench for the next day's baking."

Grandmother then understood why the carpenter, who had been a baker at one time, left his tools all over the bench, the yard, the house, the stairs and the floor. He had simply transferred his skills and his habits from baking to carpentry. She silently picked up the tools and placed them where he could find them the next day.

The kingdom of God is like a baker who scatters His children all over the earth, and at the end of the day sends His angels to gather them all together in one place. He lovingly cleans them, washes away their faults and sins, dries their tears, and if they are hurt or broken He puts them back together again. Then He gives them a piece of the cake He has baked for them.

The Man of Small Stature

Nicholas was three years old, but he understood that little people stood on stools when they needed to reach places big people could already reach. When the five-foot-six man came to his Grandmother's house to install the vertical blinds she had ordered for her windows, he stood on a stool to attach the rods. Then Nicholas understood the man was a "little man."

"My daddy is a big man," he told the man of small stature. He looked at Grandmother and said, "That man is a little man like me." The man of small stature and Grandmother laughed and exchanged praises for the boy who could make such astute comparisons.

God must seem like a very big man to a little boy, but in the kingdom of God, He gives all His children stools to stand on so He doesn't notice their height and they can see Him face to face and speak with Him at His own level.

Breaking Down Walls

Some folk say anger of any kind should not be expressed. Grandmother said there are good ways of expressing righteous indignation and not so good ways, but it's not good to repress it.

She used to tell her children to kick the door, if they must, but not each other. They said they experienced a lot of pent-up anger in those days, and Grandmother's doors suffered from the blows. She, however, never allowed herself the same privilege, that is, until she bought a townhouse.

Her sister thought it unbecoming for a fine house to have carpeted stairs, so after going 'round and 'round about it, Grandmother agreed to let her brother-in-law rebuild the stairs to the loft in pinewood. When they were finished, her sister spied the wall next to the stairway and said they ought to tear it out for storage space. Since they did not know what was behind the wall, her son, Jim, said it was not a good idea because there might be air conditioning vents or pipes behind it. So they didn't tear out the wall.

After they left, Grandmother felt frustrated because she had not made the decision, but her sister and son had, and she knew storage space was at a premium in a small townhouse where all the closets were about a foot narrower and a foot lower than most houses.

An impulse came over her to tear out the wall herself. She got a hammer and started to break through the plasterboard. With every blow she felt the frustration lift. Her confidence was restored when she saw behind the wall a shelf made from the extension of the stairs at the curve, and lovely space for Christmas boxes and suitcases. There were no pipes or anything to spoil the space.

Grandmother felt a sense of triumph and release as she phoned her sister and son to tell them what she had done. "Bravo," said her sister. "Wow, Mom, you did that?" responded her son. "You bet," Grandmother proudly replied.

When Jesus saw the moneychangers in His Father's house, He expressed righteous indignation at their actions. There is no instance in the Bible where Jesus ever hurt anyone. As Mahatma Gandhi, a very famous man, once said, "If you practice an eye for an eye or a tooth for a tooth, you will end up with a blind and toothless world."

How Do I Serve?

Yesterday I had time and strength to serve,
But, ah, God, did I love or was it youthful verve?
Today I think I know you better than in my young years,
Then I was full of fears, but now am shedding tears.
Today I wait for things less powerful than death or birth,
Today I search for truth, and to know my own worth.
Days pass quickly, uneventful into night.
Somewhere in between the dark and light,
My thoughts like silent snowflakes falter
At raindrops falling into water;
Or sunlight glittering on silver lakes
No thought of mine could ever make.
'Tis true they serve who only stand and wait,
So now I serve, and not too late.

The Bridge

It was just an old bridge, polished smooth by many feet and seasoned by the sun. The bridge held its arms open to the land on both sides, and from its hands poured humanity on its daily journey.

When it grew old and feeble, the bridge was torn down and its boards tossed in careless abandon in the grass. Then one day some builders rebuilt the bridge with brand new wood and nails. At the end of the day when they ceased their labor, one plank was found missing. Not wanting to leave the bridge unfinished, they searched the surroundings for the missing plank and found instead a section of the old bridge still intact. They took one of the weather-worn boards and lay it across the brand new bridge, easing it perfectly in place.

Then once again children walked across the bridge to school, workers to work, men and women stopped on the bridge to laugh and talk quietly about the old days, young lovers whispered their troths to each other as they passed over it, and the bridge spent its days filled with love and sunshine.

Many years passed until once again the bridge grew old and collapsed into the river. This time God Himself looked down and saw the bridge had spent its life helping people, so he raised it up, leaving one piece behind. He took the old bridge into heaven where He (who was a carpenter by trade) rebuilt it into a beautiful mansion for all his friends.

When all the people who had crossed the bridge in their lifetime came to heaven, they recognized the warm, golden color and polished boards of the mansion and were very happy to live with the bridge in its new home forever and a day.

On Line with God's Internet

Ten years before Grandmother retired and started taking care of her grandchildren, she worked as a word processor for a scientific research company. At that time she was one of only four employees in her division who operated computers. Word processing was new to the industry and not everyone had a computer. Ten years later the entire company of 5,000 employees operated a computer installed in their cubicle or office.

Today, one of the most exciting challenges for school children is to be online on the Internet. Millions of children from the United States and others countries around the world can be in touch with one another and exchange information with institutions such as zoos, businesses, libraries, scientific research companies, bookstores and places of learning.

Grandmother thought about the church as a great Internet where the people of God, and the saints in heaven can communicate with one another. She imagined she could phone St. Joseph with a carpentry problem, put him on hold politely while she phoned Nicholas and they could talk about wheels. Or she could connect with Martha and Mary about cooking recipes. Nicholas, Tiffany, Brandon, Stevie, Dawson, Kyra, Ty, Robert, Jack and Henry could have a conference call among themselves about fishing while St. Peter and St. John gave them instructions. They would discuss with Jesus how to improve their schoolwork, their relationships, or their daily prayer or spiritual life. Maybe Jesus would suggest a way to help them throw a ball better!

Then Grandmother imagined what it would be like to click the mouse and bring up an image of one of the saints or the Holy Family and have a conversation with them on the Internet. What questions the children and Grandmother would ask!

"How old are you, Jesus?"

"Mary, how did you feel when you had to ride on a donkey when you were nine months pregnant?"

Grandmother wondered why some people had a problem about talking with Mary and the saints since Jesus talked with them while on earth and still communicates with them in heaven! She thought about how Mary and Joseph spent their days on earth communicating with one another and with their Son. She thought how selfish it would be, and therefore impossible, for God not to allow His friends to speak with one another as long as they wished. It wouldn't even cost a quarter.

When Grandmother went into a bank, she reasoned, she didn't ask to see the president of the bank to get her money; she went through a teller. If she deposited her money in the bank, would the teller keep the money and not give it to the bank to earn money for her? No, she thought. Everyone has a job in heaven praising and serving God and everyone is happy doing it. Grandmother talked with all the saints, to Mary, Jesus and Joseph and asked them to help her live a good life. She also talked with the saints who do not have a saint before their names, but are living in heaven with God.

One day Grandmother went into a restaurant and when she came out, she could not find her keys. She searched and searched in her purse, dumped out the contents, but the keys were nowhere to be found.

She returned to her car and asked St. Anthony, finder of lost articles, to help her find the keys. She looked on the ground and around the car without success. Then she saw a security guard and asked him to help her find her keys.

He asked, "Did you look in your purse?"

"Of course," Grandmother replied, "when we lose something we pray to St. Anthony and then look again, and usually we find what we are looking for."

The man looked puzzled as Grandmother dug in her purse again and found her keys right where she left them in a pocket.

"See, here they are. St. Anthony won again!"

But the man only looked at Grandmother and smiled and said, "My name is Anthony."

They both laughed as Grandmother said, "Thank you, Anthony. You have a namesake in heaven."

The family of God is growing and it changes every time a new member comes into it. There is always room for one more. The family is like a great circle of hands that constantly let go in order to take other hands to make it larger. God and all the saints in heaven dance when a child is born and when anyone comes back to God who has wandered away.

"There is more rejoicing in heaven over one sheep that has been found than over 99 who have never strayed," said Jesus.

Photographs in the Attic

For over 40 years Grandmother and her sister wanted to know what their grandparents on their father's side had looked like. When her grandson and his family moved to Lawrenceville, a suburb outside Atlanta, Georgia, they got their opportunity.

As a little girl barely six years of age, Grandmother had traveled to Juliette with her mother and father to see her grandmother who was dying. Her grandmother Elizabeth had looked down on her from the old iron bedstead and smiled. Her parents had told her at the time her grandmother spoke and wrote Latin, but she had not realized what an accomplishment that was. She thought she had probably learned it as a child from her father, who was a doctor.

Driving in the old Chevy up the red clay road to the house on the hill, she remembered the old white frame house with a porch wrapped all around it. The porch was supported with large white columns in the southern style and had chickens walking around on it because Elizabeth had been too sick to shoo them away.

Returning home, the tires of the Chevy got stuck in the red clay and her father had to put boards under the wheels to pry them loose. The red clay sputtered and spat as he gunned the motor while the tires spun 'round and 'round over the old board until finally the car was freed from the mud.

When the movie "Fried Green Tomatoes" was filmed in Juliette, her cousin organized many of the townspeople to be the extras on the set. She hadn't known this, but when she saw the movie's kudos to the people of Juliette at the end of the movie, she saw a cousin's name among them. She wrote to her cousin using only his name and the name of the town of Juliette. She received a reply telling her all about the filming of the movie in which he had appeared as an extra. He also told her a cousin of hers was living in the old house with his wife. Her daughter had visited them, meeting her relatives for the first time, and took photos of the home and town and sent them to Grandmother.

On her first trip to Lawrenceville to visit her grandson Nicholas, Grandmother and the family planned a side trip to Juliette to see the old homestead. They arrived early one Sunday morning after making a phone call to cousins Dot and Bill to let them know they were coming. The cousins had confirmed there were old photographs in the attic and didn't know who they were.

When they arrived, Grandmother and her family were taken on a tour of the home and property. Then Dot invited them into the kitchen where she had prepared a sumptuous brunch for them. Just above the large round table on which breakfast was served, Grandmother saw a trap door leading to an attic. She stood in anticipation as Bill brought out old framed photographs from the early 1900s. She remembered her father had told her his dad (who died before Grandmother was born) had a drooping, red mustache. To her surprise, there was a portrait of a young man with a drooping mustache, as well as that of a young woman wearing a high collared dress with a sweet, although mysterious, smile on her face who she vaguely remembered seeing once before. She was convinced this woman, who appeared gentle and strong at once (she had 14 children), was her grandmother and the young man her grandfather. She was thrilled when Dot and Bill told her she could have the photographs. They had not known who they were.

Touring the town of Juliette, they met a couple of cousins who owned the "Whistle Stop Café" and ate two servings of fried green tomatoes, which turned out to be "red" instead of the out of season green.

Journeying to the Methodist Church (also in the movie) they viewed many of the Welsh Williams' family graves in the cemetery alongside the church. There was a small gravestone for the baby who died at one year, for a soldier who died in the war, and the grandparents of Grandmother. They took many photographs to take back with them.

When she returned home, Grandmother felt a sense of peace knowing she had grandparents of a gentle and sturdy Welsh stock, who trusted in God and one another. They never abandoned the land on which they lived. Eighty years later a daughter was born in the house, lived in it during her lifetime and then passed it down to Dot and Bill, who show it off to all who come through the town on a bus tour.

In years to come, Dot and Bill told her, they would give the home to their son who lives only a mile away. They believe he will probably sell it as he has his own home. Grandmother pictures the home as a bed and breakfast where tourists would come when visiting the town of Juliette. What stories the attic will contain for new families who discover the remaining photographs hidden there.

Rain

The June rain poured down the spout onto the sidewalk as Grandmother made her way to the car, covering herself with a golf umbrella. She fumbled for the keys, folded her umbrella and got in. Minutes before, she had gathered together some odds and ends of old jewelry and other useful items to take to her sister at the antique store where she worked. Some she had purchased and some were given to her by her sister years before when she owned another store. Grandmother thought they would be more useful to her sister now.

She started the car and drove out onto the highway. At the crossing she stopped for a red light and observed a man selling papers. As the rain continued to pour down, Grandmother wondered what kind of person would attempt to sell soggy papers in the rain. She saw his dripping wet face, his clothes soaked, and the papers folded over his arm in a lumpy mess of papier-mâché just about perfect for making puppets. Was he a homeless man who had discovered a bunch of papers and was trying to sell them for a few coins? His boldness coupled with the fact his shirt was imprinted with "The Herald" convinced Grandmother he was a genuine paper peddler. As she waited for the light, Grandmother heard a horn blow and watched in the rearview window as the man scurried over to a car and pulled out a perfectly dry paper from under the soggy bundle draped over his arm.

She felt a sense of shame as the light turned green and she drove on. How could she have passed such a severe judgment on the poor man? She wondered if she did that more than she realized. Stopping once again to pick up lunch for herself and her sister, Grandmother soon arrived at the antique store. As she looked around at the antiques she noticed the smell of mothballs hovering in the air. Her eyes finally came to rest upon her sister, soaking wet from bringing in the items from Grandmother's car. With an unexpected feeling of relief and hope, Grandmother let down her umbrella, folded it and sat down. As they ate their lunch together, she told her sister the story of the man selling dry newspapers in the rain.

A Mother's Gift

Once upon a time, not so long ago, there was a little girl who did not know she was loved. Her mother, being sick, did not hold her, kiss her, or touch her because she wanted to protect her. She didn't tell her she loved her either, so the girl didn't know what love was, what it felt like, or how it looked.

Her wonderful aunts gave her an idea of what love was when they cooked for her, took her places, bought her school clothes, or combed and curled her hair; so this is what she thought love was.

Her teachers shared their knowledge, and nature was always there for her in the beautiful Floridian town where she lived. She thought this was love, too.

One day a friend of Christ, a loving, celibate priest, hugged her hard, and it was the best hug of all because she thought this must be the way Christ would hug. But it confused her. She didn't know the feeling because as a little girl no one had told her this was love and this is how it feels and it's OK.

When she joined the church and married and had children, she held them in her arms and kissed them and told them she loved them. She thought finally she knew what love was.

Then one day the People of God began to hug and kiss one another and shake hands in church, and she caught on and returned the same. This seemed like love to her, too. One Mother's Day her pastor told a story: "What if your mother did not hold you or kiss you or touch you, but put you in a cold place and never told you she loved you. That would be terrible," he said, "you would become a monster!"

Tears fell down her face. She realized for the first time what had happened to her. She had become a monster! Oh, how could that happen? she thought. Suddenly through the tears she realized her mother had really loved her by protecting her. She knew the loving pastor had really loved her, too, by showing her the most beautiful and tender love of all—the love of a real mother.

Finally, the little girl inside the woman knew what love felt like, and she felt love from the bottom of her little feet to the top of her head. Her heart was full of God's love and tears flowed down her cheeks. The people of God shook her hand and seemed to congratulate her upon her discovery. She was loved.

City Lights

It was late afternoon. Coming home on I-95 North, Grandmother saw a tall building off to the west with a thousand shining eyes appearing out of the darkening sky. Suddenly, at the bend it loomed eastward among a multitude of similar buildings with luminous facades. They reflected the fast-descending sun as it splashed its brilliant golden-orange paint onto a deep purple canvas. Soft gray and white cloud fingers gently lowered the sun behind the horizon.

This was the city in the January winter. Traveling down the expressway homeward bound, Grandmother saw the skyline standing erect in the approaching distance, reminiscent of tall guardian angels of cities, larger than the cold-cast figurines in disappearing mangers around the city, but just as immobile. Totally unlike anything she knew of the movement of angels, they nevertheless forced her attention on the majesty of all that surrounded her.

Sometimes Grandmother wondered if Mary would come to this city at all, except to hold her child close and flee the city's grasp. Would she not fear the too-real dangers within? Yet Grandmother knew Jesus said, "Blessed are they who have not seen, but have believed."

Dots of red taillights through the misty windshield turned into streams of blood in her imagination, while dots of headlights in the rearview mirror became streams of grace, as they blended together in the rain and fell on the wet highway. She sensed Mary holding her baby closer to protect Him as she drove homeward through the city traffic surrounded by her guardian angels. Peace seemed to settle over the city as night fell.

Morning followed evening while the city slept. The rising sun reflected its rays on the building with the thousand eyes, fresh from the evening rain. The homeless awoke on street corners, in cardboard boxes and under bridges. Grandmother guessed not one of them knew Mary and Jesus had passed through on their journey and blessed them, but she believed. The one who lived with angels on Earth, the one who appeared with beauty, love and human tenderness to children, the one who lets "all God's glory through" came in hills and grottoes, lakes and cabbage patches, to La Sallete and Lourdes, Pontmain and Knock, Beauraing and Banneaux, Rue du Bac and yes, perhaps, even to Medjugorje. She appeared to those weak in faith and poor in material things, bringing riches of love and mercy to those who forever after would be filled with her memory and bring thousands into the range of God's merciful love.

$\mathcal{A}$cknowledgments

Thank you, Father, for my years of public school education, my Catholic college and university education, and teaching years. I did not meet you early in person, Father, but through nature and some very good teachers and students, I glimpsed what life with you could be like. For example, my first grade teacher, Mrs. Clark, taught me what it meant to be a part of a whole. She asked each one of us to make a portion of a farm. The silo fell to me. I made a splendid silo out of an oatmeal box. When the farm was assembled, I viewed the whole farm scene with my silo in the center, magnifying my childish efforts.

In second grade you allowed me to experience what it felt like to be head of my class, and then to fall from grace when I was forced to skip a grade and lost my position. I wanted to be the best in everything, but the effect of skipping a grade separated me socially from my peers and left me struggling to achieve. No, your name was not mentioned, but somehow I felt your presence in deep longing in my soul.

In public school I received an education that helped me earn a living as an adult. I met many of your children of all faiths, and some with no faith; rich and poor alike were present there with their "absentee Father."

When I joined the Catholic Church and taught in Catholic schools, I was finally able to meet you in person and speak with the students about you. I felt inwardly, however, that someone was missing when I looked around and did not see all of your children. I didn't see the handicapped, or the very poor, or black children at the time, or those who were "slow" and needed special instruction; nor did I see children of other faiths who also were Christians. Nevertheless, I was happy to be with you at last.

Or so I thought. When my own children were of school age, I sent them to Catholic schools where I hoped they would learn about you. When my son was in second grade, my husband became ill and I could no longer keep them in a private school, so I transferred them to a public school where I fearfully dreaded your absence. I thank you that there were religious education classes in my parish where I could volunteer to teach my own children and others about God. To my surprise, many of the teachers in my children's elementary school were not afraid to use the name of God. I counted the number of times your name was mentioned in one of the PTA meetings I attended and it totaled eight times in all by the end of the meeting!

Then I said to myself, "God must be here after all because when He walked the earth He reached out to children, spoke with them, healed them and said His kingdom was made up of them. He scolded the apostles for forbidding them to come to Him. No, Father, the name of your Son is not mentioned in the public schools, but the children there await your saving grace, and ache and long for their Father's love as much as your children in private schools.

Finally, Father, I thank you for the Catholic school and college education you arranged for my daughter. She made me proud to be her mother when she made honors and served in her parish religious education program while only a teenager, and later became the mother of Kaio and Ty. I thank you also for my son who served his country in the U.S. Navy and is now the proud father of Nicholas, Kyra and Dawson.

With humility and love I turn the religious education of my grandchildren over to you, Father. I know you will arrange it in the best way you know how.

May the Peace of the Lord be with all who read this book of stories.

About the Author

Joyce Ann Edmondson was born of Southern parents of no particular faith, but as a young girl she was introduced to Christ through her relatives and peers. At the age of 23 she became a Roman Catholic and spent 30 years in service to the church as a teacher and secretary. After Vatican II, Joyce spent five years serving her parish, St. James in North Miami, as chairperson of the Adult Religious Education Committee. The committee was active in bringing the changes initiated by Vatican II to the parish level and sponsored four programs of adult education yearly. Prior to this she served as chairman of the high school division of the Confraternity of Christian Doctrine in St. Mary's Cathedral Parish and as CCD teacher. She was also active in the Legion of Mary, a missionary organization of the church. At the age of 58 she received her B.P.S. degree from Barry University in Miami, Florida specializing in education.

After retiring from the Archdiocese of Miami, she was employed for eleven years as a word processor for Coulter Immunology, a division of the Beckman-Coulter Corporation in South Miami.

Joyce has been writing short stories and poetry for the past ten years, as well as painting pastel portraits of young children. At present she attends St. Benedict's Episcopal Church in Plantation with her husband John, a composer/arranger. Together, they have ten grandchildren.